DRAGON ESSENCE

A PREQUEL TO THE DARK AGE TRILOGY

NIAMH MURPHY

NIM PUBLISHING, 2018

Copyright © 2018 by Niamh Murphy

All rights reserved.

No part of this book may be reproduced in any form or by any electronic or mechanical means, including information storage and retrieval systems, without written permission from the author, except for the use of brief quotations in a book review.

Cover Art by Tithi Luadthong

For Louise...

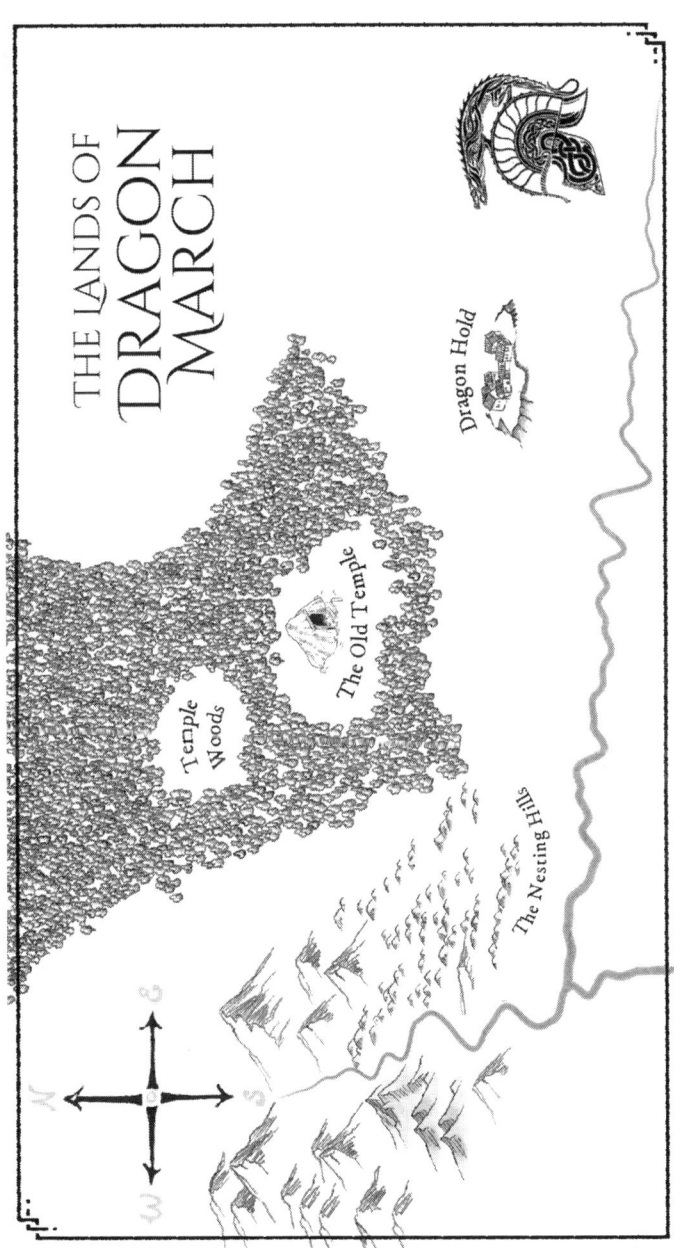

PRONUNCIATION

Myrddym - Meer-Thim
Gilde - Gild

1

WILD ONE

Andra grabbed the mage's arm, turning her back. "I'll not let you do this!"

But Olwen shook her grip loose. "There's nothing you can do to prevent me," she spat.

Olwen turned and ran down the uneven path through the dimly lit forest. The waning moon was high but little light emanated from the shining crescent, and the forest was dark and silent but for the wind rustling the late summer leaves.

Andra paced at the edge of the wood, watching the mage disappear, her red dress and long curls of dark hair vanishing into the trees. Olwen was right, there was little Andra could do to stop her, but she had to try. She reached for the hilt of her sword, a nervous habit, and was shocked to realise she was thinking of using it. She would do anything to prevent a battle, but would she go so far as to use a blade?

Andra took a deep breath.

She could just let Olwen go. Let her find the nest and desecrate it... while she returned to barracks. The mage would perform her magic ritual and Andra would pretend she had known nothing. Olwen could obtain the power she so craved, and no one would ever know of the loyal Captain's betrayal. But if it all went wrong... could she live with herself?

Her decision was made.

She drew her sword and took off at a run after Olwen. The mage was fast, but she was faster.

As a huntress she had tracked through this forest many a night: she knew every crevice, every path, and every tree root. Even in the dark, the memory of each twist and turn was enough to guide her, and she was quick to gain on the mage.

There was a flash of red cloth through the trees. Andra turned down a track and leapt over a fallen tree. Her movements were swift and quiet.

Another flash of red. It was gone in an instant but Andra hurried after it, her breath heavy in her chest.

Olwen was just ahead. She was unsure of her path and was using her magic to light the way. She was bright as a beacon in the woods. An easy target.

Andra took a side path and darted up a steep slope. She overtook the woman running on the path below then leapt down, landing squarely in front of her and blocking the way.

Olwen let out a cry of surprise. She stumbled to a halt but recovered instantly.

"I warned you, Andra. Do not stand in my way!" She raised her hand and the cloth of her sleeve fell back, revealing the dark lines of power tattooed on her forearm. The ball of blue mage-light pulsated as it swirled in her open fist before turning into a raging green orb casting eerie shadows on her features.

"I'll not let you raid that nest." Andra raised her sword.

Olwen's dark blue eyes widened in surprise. "Do you intend to strike me down, Captain?"

"I'll do whatever I have to." Andra stood firmly in the mage's path but a knot of fear was twisting her stomach. Staying loyal to the Druid people meant betraying Olwen, and, apart from anything else, Olwen could kill her in an instant.

Andra wanted to start the night again. Everything had been so different just a few hours ago: when she finished her guard shift she had been so excited to see her lover. They had agreed to meet at sunset and Olwen had promised that everything would be different after tonight. That everything would change. Andra had believed this would be the night they ran away together, the night they were finally free of their obligations. She should have known that Olwen would have a different plan.

Olwen laughed. "You know I can snap that sword in two with a mere thought."

Andra shook her head and lowered the blade. "Please," she said, holding out her hand, "I cannot bear the thought of losing you." She took Olwen's free hand in her own and Olwen dropped her magic. The light went out and they held one another in the dark. "I love you," Andra whispered.

The forest was quiet all around them. Andra could feel her lover's heartbeat against her own and the warmth of Olwen's breath against the skin of her neck. She closed her eyes, sinking into their embrace. There was no one else in the world at that moment. Nothing mattered except holding each other. She wanted to stay that way forever. Her grip tightened. "I beg you, please don't try this new magic of yours."

"I've told you, I must." Olwen pulled away and looked up at her in the dark.

"Can we not run? Go somewhere we won't be found—"

"There's no such place." Olwen shook her head. "The only language the wizards speak is power and they will not leave us alone until I am more powerful than all of them."

"Does it have to be a dragon's egg? Is there nothing else?"

"Nothing so potent."

Andra sighed and turned away. "But what if this ritual fails? If it's never been done before then how can you know the danger?" They were talking in circles, as they had done all night, repeating the same arguments over and over, yet she was compelled to make them again. She wanted to force Olwen to see things the way she did. "Is it really worth risking your life for?"

Olwen took Andra's hand and moved close. "The wizards will always keep us apart... They'll take me, Andra, imprison me on some wind-bitten solitary skerry. Isolated, no way of drawing power. No way of seeing you. I'd rather die."

"But what if Myrddym is already there? Lying in wait?"

"I have no doubt that she is."

"But you cannot face her alone."

"I will have Gilde."

"Gilde? She's nought but a shamana, what good is she?"

"You underestimate me." Olwen threw Andra's hand down and stepped away angrily.

"And you underestimate Myrddym! She is more powerful than anyone."

"She's a mad old hag." Olwen spun around, staring hard at Andra. She opened her fist and the magic tickled the hairs on Andra's neck as it glowed, making eerie shadows dance on the trees. "She will not stand in my way, Andra." Olwen raised her hand: the light was blinding, forcing Andra to raise her arm to cover her eyes. "No one will!"

"No," Andra cried, raising her sword uselessly against the light. "Don't!" She swung madly, blindly.

"There is no other way."

The light flashed, swallowing everything and leaving only a bright whiteness. Andra screamed as the white filled her senses. Her muscles stiffened. She couldn't move and couldn't see. The forest was gone and all she could hear, feel, smell and taste was the brightness of the light.

As quickly as it had come, it was gone.

Her body collapsed to the ground and she barely had time to register the woman she loved running off into the woods, before the darkness swallowed her. Then she knew nothing at all.

2

DUEL

It was still dark when Andra was roughly shaken awake. She stirred groaning and trying to distinguish the familiar voice. "Olwen?"

"Quickly, quickly." It was a broken voice of many years, with a rough northern farmer's twang. The shaking on her arm continued, almost dragging her sleeping body from the ground. "Come on, Captain, off yer arse," the voice hissed. "Myrddym was waiting."

"Gilde? Is that you?" Andra blinked but the dark was all around her. She felt as if she had drunk nothing in days, her flesh stung, and was still ringing with the aftershock as if a bell had sounded within her. She crawled up onto her knees and tried to clear the heavy fog from her mind while Gilde danced with frantic panic around her.

"She'll kill us all!" The Druid woman was wild: her old, grey eyes were wide with panic and her white braids were loosening. Stray hairs clung to the damp skin of her haggard face, weathered with a thousand concerns. Andra had never seen the old half-mage shamana like this.

Andra stood unsteadily: her sword was missing, and she

panicked searching around in the dark for it. Her boot kicked it and she felt for it in the dry leaves. "What do you want, woman?"

"That old bitch were waiting! 'Tis all we can do to run! Come, come. That's it, bring your sword; I need you armed." She dragged on Andra's arm and, with her other hand, she pulled at her tatty, faded cloak as her worn brooches failed to hold it in place.

But Andra stood stock still in the nightwood. "You abandoned Olwen?"

"Come on, stop yer tarrying, my rough magic is nothing to that old witch, you're the only protection I've got."

Andra threw Gilde off and scanned the forest. The stars were out and bright, but not enough to light her way. She would have to pick out the path from memory. She turned away, heading north. Gilde called after her but she had no time to waste: if that mad old shamana was right then Olwen was in danger.

Sheathing her sword to better run through the trees, Andra zipped along this way and that, her head clearing as she ran. She listened to the vibrant sounds of the forest at night over the heavy sound of her breathing and the soft tapping of her boots against the hard, dry ground. The trees were calm. For now.

It wasn't far, two maybe three miles through the wood and, if she was fast, she might get there in time. She knew she would have to climb the slope to reach the concealed nest of the dragon. It was a tricky climb, even in the daytime, and she would likely die if she had to face that old hag, Myrddym, but if Olwen was gone.... Well, she might as well be dead.

Andra reached the northern edge of the wood in a few minutes. She was out of breath but ready. She glanced around. The landscape was cool and blue-black against the starlit sky. The moon had gone, long fallen below the horizon, but she had no need of natural light. Above her to the right, accompanied by the prickle of magic across her skin, were the two women, a Druid and a Dwarf, locked in battle.

The sparkle and blazing of their magic lit them up like a midwinter bonfire, their silhouettes bright against their own unnatural weaponry. Olwen, tall and brave, using her own body as a weapon; the magic in her blood bursting from her palms as she threw blast after blast of blazing green light. Her foe, an old dwarven woman half Olwen's height and twice her width, in a rough-hewn robe, the hood thrown back to reveal a mass of short, dark, wiry curls, wielded a staff of wizened oak. The Dwarf deflected the blasts Olwen sent as if they were no more than clumsily tossed sods of earth.

Andra was frozen with uncertainty. It was foolish to interrupt a mage battle, madness to believe she could somehow pull Olwen away and take her to safety. She was just a guard. A fool with a sword. What good was she against a wizard? Even if it was only this mad old crone.

Suddenly, a blast of lightning from the crone's staff caught Olwen unawares and she stumbled, unable to retaliate before she was blasted again.

Her decision made, Andra rushed towards the hill, creeping nearer across the short grass of the pasture. She knew the farmers in their hut would be wide awake listening to the battle cries, filled with terror of the creatures of the night screeching and blasting just beyond their front door. She pitied them and willed them to stay inside away from this madness.

Andra checked her sword and stood with her back to the slope. Directly above her, the battle raged on. The

Dwarf was powerful but even she could be stopped. Even she could be felled if taken by surprise. A mere sword would be enough to destroy that creature if only Andra could ascend the slope and climb up behind her. She could creep up silently and shear the head clean from the crone's shoulders. Myrddym was but a Dwarf, no physical strength, her power was entirely magical. All Andra had to do was hope that Olwen kept her busy enough not to notice a Captain of the Dragon Guard climbing up behind her.

She could hear the shouts over the thunder of the magic missiles.

"—No good can come of this betrayal—" the Dwarf crone was saying. Andra shook her head; if anyone had been betrayed it had been Olwen. Betrayed by the Wizard Council. Betrayed by the very people who had raised her, taken her from her family as a child, sweetened them with promises of greatness and of learning the 'noble call' of magic. But the wizards didn't even tell Olwen when her family were killed. Didn't tell her they were even in danger, even though Olwen could have helped them. She could have prevented the tragedy.

All they wanted was to keep Olwen for themselves and make her swear an oath renouncing the Druid people, renouncing her race to become a wizard. They said she had a choice, yet when she refused they came after her, forced her into hiding. If Andra hadn't found her all those years ago, lost and starving, terrified of every shadow, then she would have died alone. No one would have even known she had gone.

As Andra watched the battle unfold she realised that Olwen was right; she wouldn't be free until all the wizards were dead. Or she was.

"The power you unleashed within me," Olwen retorted. "You cannot force me to keep it hidden."

"Not hidden, Olwen, used for good."

"The good of who?" Another great crack of thunder, repelled by a flash of bright red.

Olwen would have to defeat Myrddym in order to get past her and into the dragon's nest, but right now it looked as though she could barely hold her own against the Dwarf. Andra began an unsteady ascent of the steep hill, and she couldn't wait; Olwen couldn't hold out for long.

"You hide magic from all those who need it," Olwen shouted, and her rage vibrated on the air. "I will not hide!"

As Andra looked up she saw the flash of fire pulse through Olwen's body and erupt from her outstretched hands. For a moment it seemed as though she had caught the Dwarf full blast, that she had won, and Andra went to climb those last few feet to the crest of the slope. But the crone was not defeated. Her staff absorbed the blow of fire. She swept it around her head and blasted it back at Olwen just as she was recovering from the exertion. She was caught off guard.

Olwen flew up thirty, forty, fifty feet into the air. All Andra could do was watch as her lover soared away from the hillside then plummeted to the ground. She hit the earth with a sickening crack.

Andra swooned. Clinging to the hillside and gripping the grass between her fingers, she slid, down, down, down, back to the pasture.

She knew and yet still dared to hope.

Drawing herself up, unsteady like a drunk and fumbling in the dark, she ran toward where she saw Olwen fall and there, on the grass, her lifeless body lay.

Andra dropped to her knees.

Olwen was broken, twisted. Her neck and limbs were at strange angles and her blue eyes were wide in shock, staring forever at the death that had now passed.

It was over. Andra felt bare. Only an empty disbelief. Her body was a hollow, rattling cage holding nothing. She reached forward but couldn't bring herself to touch Olwen's skin; she recoiled and the rage boiled through her in an instant.

She screamed, yelling to the sky before pulling her sword and whirling around to the crone. "You!"

The Dwarf had followed her. How this woman had nimbly descended the slope Andra did not know, nor did she care. She stood mere feet away from Andra. Her wiry black hair was whitening at the roots, and her piercing black eyes were narrowed under a furrowed brow. She didn't waver under the point of the Captain's sword but Andra noticed her broad hands tighten on the wizened oak staff she held; its mass of roots at one end reminded Andra of a many-taloned, outstretched hand.

"I will destroy you!"

But the Dwarf crone simply shook her head sadly. "I've no quarrel with you, Druid. Take the body," she said with a wave, "and send her to your Gods." With that, she turned and was gone.

3

TEMPLE

Her knees finally buckling under the weight, Andra stumbled through the narrow entrance of the stone temple and lay the body on the ground.

A soft light emanated from the north chamber and an unearthly voice echoed around the walls. "Who doth trespass upon this ancient— By Dragon's Breath! you carried her here?" Gilde dropped the facade and rushed to kneel over the body of Olwen. Her hands glowed as she inspected the wounds.

Andra leaned against the wall, breathing hard. It stank in this place. Water collected in puddles along the narrow aisle and stagnated; it was bare like an abandoned cattle pen. She had no idea why it was such a sacred spot to the Druids, but she knew it was where she would find Gilde hiding, and the shamana was the only person she could go to now. "I... I thought you might help her."

"She's dead." Gilde's words were low, definite and brutal.

"Curse her! That—" Andra choked on the words. She blinked and swallowed but was unable to continue. Her breath was ragged. She was exhausted, body, mind and heart. She took a deep breath, focusing on the flickering of Gilde's mage-light and ignoring the still-open eyes of her lover. "There must be some potion or healing enchantment?"

Gilde sucked in the air between her teeth as if she were no more than a blacksmith inspecting a badly shoed horse. "Her neck is broken, Andra, not to mention these other wounds—"

And with that, Andra's last hope was smashed.

She suddenly straightened and let out a roar of frustration, pacing the aisle and smashing the crystals and potion bottles Gilde had collected in the North Chamber. The crashing and breaking of pot against stone echoed around the temple and, in an instant, the floor became a mass of oils, philtres, sherds and parchments.

"I will destroy her." She turned on Gilde, who shrank back across the dirt floor. "I will tear her to pieces. I won't rest until her head is atop a pike." Striding toward the entryway, Andra stepped over the frightened shamana and drew her sword. She didn't care how it was to be achieved. But she wanted to see that Dwarf crone sliced into pieces with every inch of her body rotting in a putrid ditch.

"She'll smash yer to bits, Andra!" Gilde shouted.

Andra stopped. Her fist tightly gripping the sword, she looked at the ground. Her body raged with a fire she couldn't contain. "She won't even see me coming." Andra nodded to herself and took a stride toward the temple entrance.

"Not bloody likely. That bitch won't let y' close enough to smell her farts."

"By Dragon fire, Gilde! What would you have me do?" She threw herself against the wall, wanting to smash the great stones to shattered pieces and tear every building in Dragon March to the ground. "Must I forget her? Move on? Bury–" She choked on the thought. "Bury her..." Her rage finished on a whisper and she tried to swallow the tears that ran freely. She sank to her knees on the hard, earthen floor. She wanted Olwen. Her heart was crying out for her, but the call would remain unanswered.

"There is something..." Gilde's whisper was eager, excited.

"Tell me." Andra coughed, trying to clear the sorrow from her voice. "Tell me, I'll do anything." She tried to hold back the hope, but she couldn't prevent it rising. Perhaps magic could help her yet.

"I could perform the ritual."

Andra turned, wiping her face on a sleeve. "What?"

"The Dragon Essence. It might..." Gilde heaved herself from the ground and scurried off to the North Chamber.

"But," Andra shook her head, "I don't understand, how can we perform the ritual without her? And how will it destroy Myrddym?"

"Forget the Dwarf bitch, Andra: see beyond that little hag." Gilde lit a candle and started to frantically dig around in the wrecked detritus scattered upon her precious temple floor. Her face flushed, she turned to Andra and scampered down the narrow stone aisle waving a torn piece of parchment in her hand. A strange, lopsided grin swallowed her face into a thousand lines. "There's nowt stoppin' us! Just you see."

"Nowt?" The woman was mad, grinning at her like that. Did she not see what had happened this night? "Olwen is dead. Is that not enough?"

But Gilde was chuckling and shaking her head. She waved her hand furiously. "'Tis the same, 'tis the same!"

She laughed and Andra unconsciously moved back as Gilde leapt at her, pointing at the parchment covered in strange, half-familiar symbols. Some of them had been written into Olwen's skin: they were lines of power, the language of magic. "If it works the way we had planned then there is no reason she needs to be alive at the beginning."

"At the beginning? What?" Andra glanced down at the body, misshapen with injury. She looked away quickly and shook her head. "Bring her back, you mean? You can bring her back from the dead?" Excitement, nerves, fear, a rush of emotions crawled around in her belly.

Gilde nodded vigorously. "Do you not see? No, no, a thundering brute such as yerself has no eye for the subtle veil of magic." Andra opened her mouth to retort but Gilde was a flurry of excited rambling. "Power, Andra, the power of life itself. Essence! That's what Olwen understood. That's what we were after." Gilde kneeled down to inspect the body. "You and I, and everything alive, we're all just a vessel. Like this potion bottle." She picked up an unbroken clay bottle that had rolled into the aisle and shook it. "Filled with life. But Olwen..." She replaced the unbroken bottle on the floor and trotted over to the north chamber. A moment later she returned with two broken halves. "Olwen is broken. With a little bit of magic..." Gilde pressed the clay sherds together to reform the bottle and her hands glowed as the cracks melted away. "We can put her back together, and..." She grinned and picked up the full bottle from the floor, popped the top and poured the contents into the newly repaired bottle. "... We can fill her back up!" She held up the potion with a grin of mad delight.

Andra reached out and took the empty potion bottle from Gilde. She turned it in her hand and then held it up. "But now this one has nothing left."

Gilde snatched it from her grasp. "That's why we need a bloody big bottle!"

"And... and you're certain it will work?"

"Certain as I can be... that is to say, I reckon it'll work and my reckonin' ain't too shabby." She leaned down and closed Olwen's eyes.

Andra stared. She'd never see those blue eyes again, never hear that laugh again, never hold her warm body against her. "So, you're serious, you can bring her back from the dead?" Andra whispered knowing the Gods could hear them speak.

"Aye. I can. But we need to do this ritual you were so set on preventin'. And we need it done tonight." Gilde looked up at her, her eyebrows raised expectantly and, with a sinking realisation, Andra knew that she still needed the dragon egg. The very task, the betrayal of the Gods that she had tried her damnedest to prevent Olwen from committing, had fallen upon her own shoulders.

Andra sighed and dropped her head. "And what if Myrddym—"

"Myrddym thinks Olwen is dead. She's not come here so she'll be off; gone to the Tor to gloat, no doubt."

"She won't have sealed the entrance?"

"Sealed it?" Gilde laughed. "They should've sealed that entrance long ago but greed for the dragon always prevented it. Now that danger's passed you think she'd have gone and locked up that egg for good? Well, if it be, then you can paint me blue and call me Piskie. 'Cause I'll grow feathers afore a wizard shows sense."

Andra crouched down. Olwen's cheek was cold beneath her fingers. *What would she have me do?*

"She was willing to lay down her life for this, Andra,"

Gilde whispered, reading her thoughts. "Now, are you willin' to do the same for her?"

"Death is the only thing I have left to give." She stood and sheathed her sword, before turning from the temple.

"Andra?"

She looked back at the shamana, still kneeling over Olwen. Gilde delved into one of her pockets and pulled out a small clay bottle, and she tossed it at Andra. "The cavern'll be protected."

Andra looked down at the little bottle. "What's this?"

"Spirit oil. Pour it on your sword and you'll be able to slice all the way to the next realm."

"I hope I don't need it."

"Oh, you will."

Andra pocketed the oil and thanked her. Then she turned and headed back out into the night.

4

CAVERN

It was beyond midnight and the darkness was a thick, black velvet that crushed the senses.

Andra kept her pace swift, half-feeling her way through thickets as her chest heaved. How many times would she make this journey tonight? The edge of the forest loomed ahead of her and starlight dotted the bare sky as she left the safety of the woods and crept across the pasture.

The Dwarf crone may still be about. Gilde knew the nest would be protected by spirits. But whether she had meant by the magic of the crone or enchantments left behind by the ancients, Andra had no way of telling.

She made her way toward the hill, discernible against the black night sky only by silhouette.

The air tingled with the remnants of the mage duel. This was the place, the very place she had witnessed the battle. The moment she had watched Olwen fall flashed again in her mind. It couldn't be real, surely she could not be truly dead, surely she couldn't be revived by a spell? Andra closed her eyes, wishing herself back at her barracks. She wanted to just roll over in her sleep and wake to find it all a terrible dream. She had never left to meet Olwen, Olwen had never told her of the plan to steal the dragon egg, they had never argued, she had never watched her face Myrddym alone, and never seen her fall ... but it had all happened.

Andra stood at the bottom of the slope. Listening. She could almost hear the remnants of the battle hanging in the air. But there was no one else there. She was alone. Off in the distance, she could hear a restless owl hooting for a mate. The air was still and cool.

She began climbing the slope steadily using hand and footholds that were no more than tufts of grass loose under her fingers. She had to scrabble around for them in the dark, feeling upwards blindly. Dust and mud tumbled onto her and she kept her head down to prevent the loose grit falling into her eyes. Gradually she felt her way up the slope with her belly down, sliding back occasionally but grimly determined.

Roughly halfway up the steep hill was the flattish grass plateau on which the mage duel had taken place. She allowed herself a moment to rest and find her bearings. The earth hummed with the recent use of magic. Her skin tingled, and her ears filled with the soft, distant yet full sound. Was it even a sound? It was a feeling that she could hear throughout her whole body. Yes. That was the only way she could describe it. She could almost see the blackness of the night vibrating. She crawled along on her knees, feeling for the edge to prevent falling while she crept toward the place where the magic was at its thickest. The opening was here.

A crack in the rock almost invisible to the untrained eye. It was known only to the Wizard Council and Officers of the Druid Dragon Guard. It was a place so sought after by so many and yet here it was: a nondescript crack in a rock-face on a hillside overlooking a small farm west of nowhere.

Andra felt a pang of guilt.

This was all her fault.

Olwen would never have known of the sacred nesting place of the White Dragon if she hadn't been told of it by a lovelorn Captain of the Dragon Guard. If Andra had never told Olwen that, for the first time in living memory, the Great White Dragon of Dragon March was preparing to lay, then Olwen would never have devised the ritual. She would never have even wanted the accursed egg.

Andra stood nervously at the entrance. The crone could be waiting just inside. Silently she slid her sword from its sheath and fumbled for the oil. With one hand she popped the cork and poured the contents over the blade, carefully sliding the oil over every inch of bronze before tossing the empty bottle aside.

Nothing happened.

The sword remained the same as it ever was. If this truly was a blade that could cross realms and strike a blow against a spirit, it certainly didn't look like it.

She was as ready as she could ever be.

The humming of magic inside the cavern was intensified. The air was warm, humid and a little hard to breathe but she was thankful to be out of the night. She hadn't realised how the cold had bitten at her until she was relieved of it.

The ground was soft beneath her feet with loose, dry mud or sandy silt, she couldn't be sure. In the pitch black, running her hand along the wall, she was surprised to find an unlit torch. She went to pull it from its position and hesitated.

It was dangerous. Myrddym could be waiting and

would see the light. But at the same time, she could be inside a labyrinth of tunnels and she could not afford to get lost. Hastily she lit the torch with her flints and it flickered and puckered into life. The cave was much like Gilde's temple, only this place had not been formed by human hands.

It was said that, generations ago, ancient magic wielders moved the earth to form a pathway to the dragon nest, supposedly to care for the abandoned eggs left within, but now Andra knew better. Those first wizards had wanted to steal the eggs, as they steal everything. And now Andra was here to continue that legacy of theft.

She sighed.

Dragons always left their nests. Abandoning their offspring to providence. Yet despite all her oaths of allegiance and all her years of service to the dragon, she was taking advantage of the creature's trust to fate.

A narrow tunnel fell away into a blackness that the light from her torch could not penetrate. Nevertheless, she found the firelight a comfort in the overwhelming dark. She sidled along the pathway and was relieved when, after minutes of steady descent, she reached the nesting chamber.

It was a circular cavern large enough for a horse to turn but still far smaller than she had expected. Above her, the cavern opened to the stars. It would have been a treacherous climb in and out for those first hardy mages, but not so tricky for the Great White Dragon blessed with a wingspan of nearly a hundred feet. Andra could imagine the creature squeezing backward into the nest to dig a hole in the warm earth with her feet where she would lay her egg before crawling back up into the sky.

Sheathing her sword and standing the torch in the loose, sandy floor, she felt around the loose earth for something.

Anything. The dark, sandy soil was hot, almost burning her fingers. She wasn't quite sure what the egg would look like, or even how large it would be. It's got to be in here. Gently she brushed back the dirt, then began digging harder as she started to panic.

Perhaps this was the wrong place after all. Or perhaps that accursed Dwarf had seen fit to take it to a safer place. Faster and faster she flicked up the earth like a dog desperate to claw back its buried bone until she stopped suddenly.

"By the Gods."

Three smooth, white spheres, like the crowns of skulls, sat snuggly in the hot ground. Andra breathed hard. A Dragon's nest. No one but a mage had ever come this close, not even an officer of the Dragon Guard was permitted this sacred sight. She reached out, uncertain, and grabbed hold of a single egg.

A flash of light made her jump. Holding the egg against her chest, she turned and was thrown hard against a wall. Dazed, she looked around for her attacker. The cave was empty except for a golden light, brighter than her torch.

Andra pulled herself to her feet and drew her sword. It was useless against pure magic but it was all she had. She hoped Gilde's oil was enough.

A softly shimmering golden haze of light blocked her path back. Before her eyes, the haze cast itself into the sharp-taloned form of an ancient dragon. Its jaw wide, its teeth sharp, and its tongue licking the humid air. It was a Spiritwatcher. An ancient dragon-wraith guardian.

Andra had never seen such a thing, only heard of them from legend.

She charged at it with her blade, slicing through the air. Her sword clanged against the far wall and the zing of the metal chimed around the cavern but the Spiritwatcher had gone.

Suddenly she was thrown forward, smashing her chest against the wall. The egg crumpled under her weight. Damn. She was covered in bright red egg goo. She swirled around as another apparition burst toward her. Her blade swished through it and disrupted its presence long enough for her to leap over and grab another egg. She didn't wait for the Spiritwatcher to come back. She abandoned the torch and sprinted back through the tunnel toward the entrance. As she reached the threshold she felt the rush of the Spiritwatcher against her back.

She screamed in surprise as it toppled her off her feet and over the edge of the slope.

Andra braced herself as if thrown from a horse and grunted as she landed hard with a thud on the soft pasture. Rolling and rolling, she splayed out on the ground.

She panicked and checked the egg.

It was safe. The smooth, white shell of the sphere was perfect and uncracked. Her shoulder and hip had taken the brunt of the fall, but she was alright.

She laughed and kissed the dragon egg before rising to her feet and growling in agony as she put weight on her left side.

Dammit.

Her injury would slow her down and there were only a few hours left until dawn.

5

ESSENCE

Andra burst into the stone temple. She was limping, sweat poured from her brow, and her chest was covered in thick red liquid. "I have it!" She leaned heavily against the chamber wall, out of breath, and glad to be done.

"What took you so long?"

"Wraiths."

The old shamana nodded. "Warned yer." Gilde snatched the egg from Andra and began muttering to herself as she inspected it. "Good, good, now, we must hurry, there are precious few hours afore dawn."

"And what happens then?"

Gilde looked up at her, those grey, bushy eyebrows raised. Andra hated that about her. She expected everyone to know the ways of mages, wizards and shamanas as if magic came as naturally to every Druid as breathing. "Her spirit will rise up with the sun, Andra, there'll be no coming back after that."

"Then let's get on with this ritual?"

"'Course! Just as soon as we get there." Gilde muttered

incantations to the egg before slipping it into a cloth bag slung across her body.

"Get where?"

"To yonder Dragon, o'course." Gilde turned away and shook her head as she continued to pack away bottles and ink. "Any one'd think yer skull were as thick as yer thighs."

"Dragon? What Dragon? Damn the skies, Gilde! I've brought you the egg. If we've so little time, then do the damned ritual now!"

She tutted. "You've not a notion."

"No! I don't. I had no part in any of this ritual making. You wanted dragon essence, I gave you dragon essence. What more can you need?"

Gilde growled and turned back to Andra. "This egg..." She took it from her bag and waved it about. "...is only good for one thing. It's our key. We use this to open the gateway, pop the top on the potion bottle, if y'like. But there ain't enough in this to bring girlie back to life, there ain't enough in this thing to fix a broken finger." She sighed and replaced the egg in the bag. "We need a big laddie."

Andra did not like the way this was going. "You mean we have to use an actual living dragon?"

"O'course I mean a bloody dragon, we're not likely to get the essence of dragon from a flaming goat! Now, come on, we'll take the body in me cart."

"Which dragon?"

Gilde sighed heavily. "'Which dragon?' she asks. Captain of the Dragon Guard asks 'Which Dragon?' Well, I thought we'd take a trip a hundred miles west to the Black Mountains, and visit the forge of the Red Wyvern. Which bloody dragon do y'think?"

Andra reached out to the wall to steady herself, a wave

of light-headedness threating to topple her. "You cannot mean the White Dragon." She shook her head. "I have sworn to protect—"

"It won't be the first oath you've broken tonight."

"I'm one of the Dragon Guard, Gilde, I can't just walk into there and—"

"Yes y' can, Andra, precisely because you are a Dragon Guard. Anyone else would be killed for even thinking of breaking into Dragon Hold. But you? You've got the run of the place. Right, if you ever want to see this one alive again we leave now."

Andra hesitated. She felt sick. She turned and looked back at the body. Gilde had wrapped Olwen tightly in a white shroud. It didn't seem to be her at all. It was something else: a thing. Not a person at all. But she was in there. The woman she loved. Still and slowly decaying.

Olwen was dead, and Andra needed to betray everything she stood for in order to bring her back.

"If you want to leave her dead then we'll have t' burn body afore the sun rises." Gilde took off her cloth bag and began unpacking her apparatus. "We don't want to have to cope with a wraith possession. They like mage corpses." She tutted. "It'll be a bloody mess, I can tell yer."

"No!" Andra held up a hand to stop her. She couldn't burn her. She couldn't let Olwen go. She had to do it. But even now she had a duty. "Will you... will you have to kill it?"

"In truth..." Gilde blew through her lips like an indignant horse. "I know not. Enough essence for a single human.... I doubt a great dragon would even notice... but then it ain't never been done afore..."

Andra let out a growl of frustration.

"Every moment we delay only makes it more difficult. The further her spirit wanders from her body, the harder it'll be to bring her back. And the harder it will be on the dragon."

"Is there no other way?"

"No other way to bring her back from the dead, you mean?" Gilde laughed and the sound echoed around the narrow temple walls. "No one has ever even attempted it this way! She and I were the first to even think of drawing on Dragon Essence. The wizards are all too bloody scared of their own shadows to try anything close to this kind o' magic and you think there are other ways?" She threw up her arms. "Maybe. Maybe there are! Maybe there are a thousand ways to raise the dead. To bring life back to where it's left. To pluck her spirit from the air, fix her body, and reignite her soul."

"But in all of human history, this will be the first attempt I know of that has a hope of succeeding. And this ritual has taken us years of research, of dedication. Do you have any idea how many nights, how many hours she and I have poured over inscriptions, performed rituals, how many times we have failed so we could find even a glimmer of hope that we might break through to the Dragon Realm?"

"So, to put it bluntly, Andra, no: I do not believe that between your thick head and mine, we can come up with another way to revive the dead in the few hours we've got left afore sunrise. Do you?"

"I'm sorry."

"I should bloody well think so." Gilde turned and continued muttering angrily. "Another way!" She turned back and pointed accusingly at Andra. "You shame that girl by even suggesting it. The most powerful mage of our generation dedicates years of her life to researching the Dragon Essence and you think we can just come up with somethin' else on a whim." She went back to flicking through broken items on the floor of the chamber, shaking her head. "We are to just sit here, then, are we? 'Til your indecision renders all decisions useless?"

"She is the most powerful mage of our generation, isn't she?"

"Well, she was, now look at her. No more 'an a corpse in a rag."

Gilde's callous words burned into Andra. If she followed this path then she had no idea what the outcome may be. Olwen could remain dead and the people of Dragon March would be left to face the wrath of a betrayed dragon. A dragon Andra had sworn loyalty to, a sacred dragon that was worshipped in every town and village and household in the land.

Yet if she did nothing. If she hid here, stayed away, refused to move, then... she would be burning a body come dawn.

"I promised her once that I would never hold her back," she whispered, thinking of the last illicit night that had spent together, Andra sneaking out from barracks, Olwen pursued, as always, by the wizard council. "Yet, tonight it seems that is all I have done." All the promises the two of them had made to one another... they all lay broken before her.

Gilde sniffed and shrugged.

She looked at the unfamiliar figure in the shroud. It would burn like a yule log. Her pale skin, her flesh crackling on a fire. She couldn't do it. Not while there was a flicker of hope in the darkness. She had to reach out for that hope with all the strength she possessed. She had to do everything in her power to bring her back. "I'll do it."

As soon as the words were half-formed on her lips Gilde was up and out of the temple calling back. "Let's load up the cart!"

6

DRAGON HOLD

It was quiet and cold. Andra stared up the great circular building from which the Druid fort of Dragon Hold took its name. Already the tallest building for miles, the Dragon Hold was raised upon an earthen mound. Three tiers high, the building had a further two tiers within its sloped roof and, at the peak of the thatch, a trail of grey smoke could be seen against the black sky.

Andra had spent her whole adult life guarding this building and the people within it. From a lowly apprentice of fifteen, Andra had spent the next ten years working her way up through the ranks: standing guard in the public chamber, taking duties guarding the corridors beneath, escorting Ealdormen up to the Council chamber, and, she remembered well, taking her turn on the long night watch at the foot of the steps leading up to the entrance. Marching on the spot, clapping her hands together to try to work some heat into her bones, anything to drive out the bitter cold even on a late summer night such as this.

As Andra hid in the gloom, watching the two guards on duty, their shadows distorted by their own lamps, she could easily imagine herself as either of them. Both figures had their heavy, woollen cloaks wrapped tightly around them and their woollen hats pulled down hard on their heads. A waft of hot breath occasionally broke the air in front of them. It was the last hour before sunrise: the coldest, longest hour of night watch. It was when the stars seemed to move at their slowest through the sky.

Andra could hear the clatter and restless movement of cattle in a pen behind her but, for the most part, the fort of Dragon Hold was quietly awaiting the new day.

She took a deep breath. She would delay no longer. If she was going to break into the Dragon Hold, it had to be now.

She turned and paced once more. Wishing there was another way, and knowing there wasn't. She shook her head, set her jaw, and marched boldly toward the guards.

It was an unusual hour for an off-duty visit and she was ready to be questioned. Why are you out at night? Where have you been? Where are you going? Why is your uniform torn and your armour bloody and tarnished?

Andra had snuck out of Dragon Hold many times but this was the first time that she was sneaking in. She tried to keep her eyes averted, concentrating on the building, and hoping that without eye contact she would avoid having to speak, for she knew well her voice would likely tremble.

But she faltered.

As she passed the first guard he called to her. She knew his voice and her eyes darted to meet his. It was a young recruit, eager. What was his name? Her insides had frozen, and she could not have spoken if she had wanted to.

He nodded in greeting.

She nodded back, then trotted up the steps. Doing all she could to avoid running up at full speed.

At the top of the stone steps was the entrance itself. Extended from the main building and with two storeys of balcony stretching above her to the peaked roof. The two heavy, wooden doors were closed for the night and a single guard was on duty. They leant heavily the wood, arms folded, heads down, their spears tucked under the crooks of their arms. Asleep? Surely not a Dragon Guard.

"Soldier!" Her voice was firm and brimming with confidence after her first victory.

It worked. The guard was startled awake and Andra shook her head, feigning disapproval at the lack of discipline. She opened a heavy door and let herself into the dark, torch-lit entrance hall of the Dragon Hold.

She glanced around. The light from the wall sconces was dying out. They wouldn't last much longer, just enough for the change of guard. This was the weakest point in the defences: before a fresh guard but while the night watch were reaching their lowest ebb. She hoped this would mean she could sneak all the way in without being noticed. Her confidence growing further with each step, she entered the large public chamber. The light was barely lifting the room from shadow, and she sighed with relief when she realised it was empty. She allowed herself a moment to smile. Perhaps the Gods approved after all.

Silently, as if stalking prey through the woods, she peeled off to the right and through the heavy door into the stairwell.

Another torch lit the way down the narrow stone steps all the way to the bowels of the hold. Down and down two, then three, then five flights deep until she was far down in the hillside on which the whole fort of Dragon Hold perched.

Another door blocked her path. She had never visited

the hold at night and tensely reached out to try the lock: it was unlatched. Relieved, she slid through.

"Who goes there?"

She froze and turned, peering into the darkness. She should have known that the most eager of guards would be on duty within the hold itself. She should have thought up some excuse beforehand and prepared a reason for a sudden night visit.

"'Tis Captain Andra of Blackridge." She walked straight toward the guard but he stood fast, waving his spear fiercely in her direction.

"What business have ye?"

"'Tis is not for a mere lad to know a Captain's business."

"I'm no 'mere lad', I'm a Dragon Guard. 'Tis my duty to know the business of thems who wish to enter the hold."

"I've had the likes of you sent to the whipping post for less—"

His free hand was edging toward the rope of the alarm. The slightest touch would sound the bell far above and summon all the Dragon Guard her way. There was no time. No time for rationalising. No time to second-guess herself.

Andra had drawn her sword and plunged it deep into the young man's side before he'd even blinked. He stared up at her as his knees buckled. His pike clattered to the ground as he silently opened and closed his mouth. She let him fall to the flagstone floor and stared at him for a moment. Ewen of Lindum. She had known his father. Good Druid family. Loyal to the Dragons. Loyal to the Guard. And now his blood stained the floor of the hall of Dragon Hold.

She shook her head and forced herself to look away. What had she done? What had she become? She would have died by his side before sunset and now... Now she was his murderer.

She shouldn't have been there. She should not have done it.

She sank to her knees, looking down at the boy. Just a few years older than she had been when she joined. But there was no way to save him now.

Unless...

If the ritual worked. If between them she and Gilde could revive Olwen with dragon essence, then why not the boy? Why not everyone? No one would ever have to die again.

She knew then. She finally understood why Olwen had been so determined to seek this power. Why she had been so angry at the secrets the Wizards held back. So much pain. So much suffering. And it could all be stopped by using the power of the dragons.

There was no need for regret now. She cleaned her sword and slinked off down the corridor, finding the small, heavy door of the main hold. It was locked and bolted, but for a Captain of the Dragon Guard this was no obstacle. The metal of her brass key clanged in the hollow corridor as she opened the locks and slid inside.

The hold was hot. The air was stifling with the pungent smell of putrid breath. It reminded her of the nest in the cavern. She could hear the beast breathing, but even the soft breath of dreams from a dragon was like the pounding of a thousand drums. The walls vibrated with the low growl of the exhale. Or was it the vibration of magic that the creature exuded? She didn't know.

She glided silently down the stone steps. The creature, its head the size of a full-grown bull, was coiled and sleeping like a pup. Its pearlescent white scales shone in the light of the scattered wall sconces. She was surprised that they would leave the torches lit through the night but surmised that it would be dangerous for even the White Dragon of Dragon March to be left in complete darkness.

Memories are long.

Evading its great talons and teeth, Andra took down the ancient chains from the walls that had remained unused for a hundred years. That had been a more barbarous time. The irony of her own thought bit at her as she clamped the chains closed on the creature's four paws. The neck was more difficult, and the dozy creature stifled a breath. Then woke.

Its head drew up, turned, and, with its lazy, half-closed eyes, the Great White Dragon looked directly at her.

7

THE RITUAL

Andra's mind whirled.

A thousand thoughts screamed through her head at once, and she knew the dragon could hear them all. So close to the beast she would be almost shouting her intent in its face. She muttered a prayer of love, forcing herself to think of Olwen. She was helping Olwen. That was all and nothing more. Her actions were out of love not hate. Like a mantra, she repeated her thought over and over. But it was not enough: she knew deep in her heart that she was betraying the dragon. And because she knew, the dragon knew.

Suddenly it jerked back. A hiss emanated from its mouth and the chains upon its limbs rattled. The ancient creature turned to look at them, mystified, and she took her chance, clamping the rusted chain around the creature's neck. It twisted as she tried to close the rusted metal, swinging her body this way and that. Her arms encircled its neck, her hands fumbled with the lock, and her legs gripped the beast as it let out a piercing shriek.

The lock clamped shut, she was thrown off the creature

and slammed her back into the far side of the cavern. The dragon pulled the chain. She didn't know if it would hold; she could only trust that it would.

She darted behind the beast as it tried to stand but fell back to the ground. Its limbs were too restrained. It wailed and huffed as she removed the bars, one by one, from across the two large, wooden doors that opened into the ditch directly under the palisade. Once opened, the doors were large enough to allow the dragon to come and go. But once closed, they were as impossible to break through as the main gates of the hill fort.

Andra pulled the door open and, waiting beyond, in the pitch blackness of the ditch, was Gilde. As she and her cart rolled through the open door she glanced at the white dragon and gasped in awe.

It was one thing to see the dragon sweeping over the city; it was quite another to walk into its inner sanctum and see the rise and fall of its chest as it squawked and choked, its throat constrained by the neck clamp.

"Dragon's blood," Gilde whispered, the hint of a smile at the corner of her mouth.

"Let's be done with this."

The dragon's nostrils flared, and it strained against the chains.

"There is little time." Gilde hurried about and began pouring a crimson powder from a pouch to form a circle on the ground. "Are all the doors sealed?"

Andra pulled her eyes away from the dragon and pushed closed the door, replacing the heavy, wooden bars. She glanced over to the entrance to the building above. Had she locked it when she came in?

"Place her here, Andra! Quickly."

She hurried back to Gilde and lifted Olwen's body carefully from the cart, then lay her gently in the centre of the circle of crimson powder. Gilde lit four candles and placed them around the circle. Each burned with a different colour flame; one for each of the mortal elements. Andra pulled the sword from her belt and sliced through the shroud; there was no time for careful unwrapping. Olwen's skin was white and cold, the body stiff and broken. It was a desperate hope. There was no power on earth that could inflame those cheeks and uncrack those bones. This was madness.

"Move away! Move away!" Gilde harried her from the circle and tided the crimson line where Andra had trampled through it. Then she held up a goblet to the dragon and a soft, white smoke trailed off the contents like a fog. The dragon snorted and let out a second roar. Andra backed away. She had never seen a dragon harm a human, but she had never heard a dragon make that sound.

The door! She hadn't checked it. She rushed up the stone steps and placed a wooden beam across it. She heard distant shouts beyond. The dragon must have finally roused the guards. They would discover the body of Ewen. They would be rushing toward this door at any moment.

How long would it take them to send a squadron through the ditch to the dragon door? Too long. It would be this entrance they would focus on.

Gilde began chanting and the dragon pounded its feet against the ground. Its nostrils flared wildly, and the chains shook. It would pull them loose from the walls.

Andra darted back down the steps, sword in hand, unsure of what she was going to do, but knowing she had to be ready. She pulled on the chain around the dragon's neck. It resisted and turned its golden eyes toward her. The focus of pure energy in her direction was overwhelming. Her skin tingled, and she could feel its breath against her body. She pulled the chain harder, lowering the dragon's head to the ground and restricting its movements. Gilde couldn't be distracted by the teeth and talons of a flailing dragon.

"How much longer?" Andra called through gritted teeth. The dragon was barely resisting, but it was still almost more than she could control.

The door at the top of the steps banged. There were shouts beyond it of at least two guards. Most likely there were more on the way. The alarm sounded, a peeling of bells constant and urgent many floors above.

"Gilde?" Andra urged.

"You won't hurry me by yapping."

With one hand, Gilde placed the goblet on the ground at her feet and went to her cloth bag to retrieve the egg. Andra gave a tug on the dragon's chain and pulled its head further toward her. She couldn't risk it seeing the egg and discovering that they had its precious offspring. But as soon as the thought entered Andra's mind the dragon pulled hard and turned to look at Gilde, just as she cracked it open.

The contents, fire-red and smooth, poured into the goblet and the dragon screeched. Andra fell to the ground as the dragon yanked its head away from her. The chain snapped and rebounded against Andra's face with a flick of fiery hot pain. She screamed in agony as the dragon reared its head and roared.

"What have we done?"

8

DRAGON GUARD

There was no turning back.

The guards were against the door. The dragon was flailing and flaring.

There was no way out, no way to return. She would die here, or she would do something.

The pain in Andra's cheek was staggering but she pulled herself up from the sandy floor of the cavern. The roar of the dragon, its chain flailing this way and that, and its feet stomping, was all she could hear.

She leapt forward and grabbed the swinging chain. She held it tight with both hands, gripping with all the strength in her arms as she was pulled this way and that. The beast was ferocious but, even now, when its teeth and talons could have sliced through her or Gilde like butter, it would not strike a Druid.

Gilde was oblivious as she continued to mutter her ritual. She dipped a finger into the goblet and used the bright red dragon yolk to draw lines of power on Olwen's body. She had stretched out the mage's arms and legs so that the tip of each limb reached the edge of the crimson circle, then she darted around, drawing the symbols carefully upon the exposed skin, already covered with a maze of tattoos, mumbling and muttering as she did.

There was a crash at the top of the stairs. A battering ram. It would not take them long to break down that door, just a few moments more. Could she hold them all off? Perhaps. Perhaps a few dozen at most. The stairs were narrow, as was the hallway beyond. She couldn't be rushed by more than one or two at a time.

Andra looked around in a panic. Her sword was on the ground not three feet from her, and the dragon's head was pulled down almost to the ground. She couldn't let go of the dragon. She couldn't leave the stairs undefended.

"Gilde!"

Andra needed the help of a shamana now more than ever; even a rough protection spell could be enough. But Gilde ignored her and the pounding on the door continued.

"Pull the head over."

"What? Gilde, they are about to break in."

"Forget that lot. Pull the head directly over here."

It was difficult to forget the pounding on the door. She heard the wood splinter, but did as Gilde demanded and dragged the dragon's head to rest almost directly over Olwen. As close as she could get without standing directly in the circle.

Again, Gilde held the cup up to the dragon and its body recoiled but Andra did her best to hold it in place. Then Gilde turned back to Olwen. She placed one hand on her neck and it glowed with Gilde's familiar rough magic, then with her other hand, she poured the dragon egg mixture into Olwen's open mouth.

At that moment, the dragon screeched, and the door burst open. All at once the guards poured down the stairs.

Andra let go of the chain, grabbed her sword from the ground, and ran up the steps to meet the first guard. He was eager and unskilled. She dispatched him immediately and with him, she brought down the second.

As, one after the other, she tackled the oncomers she could feel the prickle of magic in the air: the room had changed and the dragon was no longer screeching. Suddenly, as she threw yet another dispatched guard from the stone steps and onto the earth below, the next guard paused to stare behind Andra. The other guards clattered to a halt, their mouths agape, and Andra couldn't resist. She turned and, as she did, an almighty crack like a thunderbolt echoed around the room.

A light. A light so bright it was as if all the stars of the night sky were focused on the point between Olwen's body and the dragon. Gilde was crouched between them and held the right hand of Olwen against the snout of the frozen beast. Its eyes were wide, its tail stuck straight up in the air, its wings folded awkwardly around its four chained limbs, and yet not a scale on its back wavered in the light.

Andra's mouth was agape. Of all the things she had seen this night, she had not even imagined this vision before her. Gilde moved back and, to Andra's shock, Olwen's hand stayed where it was, fixed to the snout of the dragon as her hair ruffled in a breath of wind that no one else felt.

Then her eyes opened.

Andra rushed down the steps. "Olwen!"

Gilde was there in an instant. With both hands upon her breastplate, she stopped the Captain from taking a further step toward the woman who was miraculously returning to life. "Do not interrupt!"

"But she is alive!"

"No." Gilde turned back to look at the body of Olwen on the ground, moving and yet still unliving. "She is not."

The light flickered out in an instant. Olwen's hand fell to the ground and the dragon collapsed with a wailing cry. Its body was exhausted and it could barely raise its head before it collapsed again, unmoving. The guttering lights from the torches were all that were left, and the room seemed blindingly dark.

It was over.

And Olwen was still dead.

"Captain."

Andra whirled around with her sword raised and met the fearsome faces of a dozen Dragon Guards, each one armed and ready to kill her where she stood.

9

SACRIFICE

There were twelve of them.

But they were mere guards: young, inexperienced, tired from night watch, and dressed in the rudimentary leather armour of novices, while she had the experience and bronze plating of a Captain. She could take them. She was sure she could.

But the alarm was still peeling. The Dawn Guard, bright and ready for duty, would soon join them, and there nothing was worth fighting for if the ritual had failed.

She held her sword out and the guards held their ground. They didn't want any more conflict than necessary. Especially with a superior officer.

"Repeat the ritual."

Gilde stood next to her, ready to fight with a weak spell causing her fingers to glow. "The dragon's drained, Andra. It has to rest."

"We don't have time for it to take a nap."

"Stand down, Captain." A plucky guard stepped forward with her sword at the ready and her chin raised. She reminded Andra of herself at sixteen.

"You stand down. And lower your sword when addressing a superior officer!" Andra's tone made the girl falter, she stepped back, and her sword wavered, but she held it fast. She was uncertain and wouldn't take much to outmanoeuvre. But there were more behind her and more on the way.

"I've no clue what'll happen." There was a note of panic in Gilde's voice and she was not like her usual cocky self. But they had come this far and there was no other way.

"No one ever does."

At that moment, the young guard took her opportunity and swung her sword, taking Andra by surprise. But she was no match for the veteran Captain. A quick swing, then a feign to the right, followed by a sharp elbow jab to the temple, and the young woman crumpled.

But two more eager guards charged, and others leapt from the steps to take her on. She was quickly surrounded but Gilde had restarted the ritual. Andra couldn't let even one pass that crimson line. All she had to do was hold them back until Gilde finished.

Andra was fast. She responded only to attack and pulled a guard off his feet then threw another to tumble into the others. She manoeuvred around to try to see the ritual. She needed to know what was happening. Another guard came at her as she saw Gilde pour the rest of the goblet down Olwen's throat.

Suddenly the guards halted. They all turned to look in the same direction at the sound of a thunderous crack. The dragon cried out with a vague whimper. No one moved as Olwen's body rose. Her hand was fixed to the dragon's snout, and her eyes were glassy.

"Olwen?"

There was no response.

The air in the room began to change. Even the guards could feel it; they started moving away and one went clumsily to ascend the stairs backwards. All were transfixed by the light emanating from Olwen's palm upon the dragon.

The light began to grow, filling the room with piercing, bright whiteness enough to make the skin tingle and burn. Andra raised her hand to cover her eyes.

"What's happening?" More guards had descended the stairs and more would come.

"She's alive." Andra stepped forward, ignoring Gilde who tried to hold her back. Olwen was moving, she was definitely moving. Her hand was fixed upon the dragon's snout, and her eyes were blinking in the blinding light.

"She's taking too much from it, Andra... The dragon... It can't."

The dragon was in pain. Its body was like a thousand snakes squirming in a barrel. Its whole body writhing, its eyes open wide, its mouth agape, and its tongue slack. Olwen was killing it.

"Can you stop her?" Andra turned to Gilde, the empty goblet still in her hand.

"I—I don't know..." She stepped forward, but the moment she reached the crimson line her whole body was blasted backwards. Andra rushed to her while the guards stood still. Transfixed.

"Do something!" Gilde grabbed at her tunic. "Quickly! The balance of life will be lost!"

Andra didn't fully understand but, from the fear on Gilde's face, she knew she couldn't let it happen.

She ran back to the dragon: its body was still flailing wildly. "Olwen!" The figure before her didn't move. She didn't even know if it was her, if it was alive, or if there was anything of the woman she loved inside the figure sucking the life essence from the dragon she had sworn to protect.

The dragon was dying. She was sure of it. Whatever this was, she had to stop it. There was no choice.

She leaned forward and grabbed Olwen's wrist where her hand reached beyond the crimson line. The skin was hot. Andra gulped. She didn't know if she was about to save them both or kill them.

She pulled Olwen's hand, wresting her grip from the dragon, and yanking her whole body from the circle.

With a crack of thunder, the light was gone. The dragon cried out, roaring in pain. Andra was thrown to the ground and Olwen landed next to her with a soft cry.

She rushed to her and turned her on her back. Her body was warm, her flesh was pink, her pulse was racing, her body no longer broken, and her eyes flitted open, they were tinged with gold.

"Olwen, Olwen, my love?"

"Andra?"

"You're alive!" Andra pulled the woman, the living, breathing woman into an embrace, clutching her tightly against her as the dragon thrashed in its corner. The guards were now attempting to calm it and two of them pulled at the chain around its neck as it lashed at them and loosened the other chains from the walls. But the Dragon was alive. Olwen was alive. The ritual had worked. It had all worked beautifully.

"What's happened?" Olwen tried to look around and Andra helped her up from the floor.

There were guards everywhere and more were rushing in by the second. They were all heading straight for the dragon, ignoring the Captain and her lover completely.

Andra held Olwen. Her eyes were different, golden, but

everything else was the same, exactly as she had been before, and she looked up at Andra filled with trust and confusion. "Where are we!?"

"It's alright." Andra gripped her tightly. She knew they had to leave and they should go now, while the guards were too busy to notice.

Olwen turned and looked at the dragon. Her eyes widened as more than two dozen guards fought with it, trying to calm it and hold it still. "What happened here?"

Andra opened her mouth to reply but at that moment the ground shook. The dragon froze, its ears back, its lips drawn up baring its teeth, and its ferocious gaze fell upon Gilde who was struggling to gather her things together. Everyone shrank back and suddenly she screamed.

A halo of golden light burst from her, surrounding her for a moment as her scream filled the air and seemed to tear her apart. Her body was outstretched, each limb reaching painfully far. She rose, inches from the floor, floating impossibly for a moment and then the dragon breathed in the golden aura, wrenching her life essence from her. Then she fell to the floor in a heap.

Before anyone could react, the dragon had turned on one of the guards. There was the same impossible pose and the aura of golden light. Then they were dead, and another was screaming.

Guards pulled their swords. Not in two generations had there been a reason to attack a dragon, yet now they went at it with blade and spear. All oaths of protection were forgotten in an instant. With a thrash of its claws, it knocked half a dozen of them down and killed another by smashing them against the wall.

Then another golden aura was consumed.

Andra stood watching, her mouth agape, her hand on her sword, wanting to help but knowing she shouldn't.

"The ritual..." Olwen whispered next to her and it was enough to draw her attention away. "The dragon is taking back its essence."

Andra grabbed her around the waist and ran, guiding Olwen to the steps, pushing past yet more guards flooding in, and squeezing through the tight passageway toward the door.

The corridor was cool, the alarm bell still rang in the distance, guards were yelling upstairs, and two more rushed toward them along the narrow hallway toward the chamber.

"It's gone mad," Andra said, pointing back. "They can barely tame it."

The guards nodded to her, not suspecting her crimes for a moment, and she took Olwen's hand, pulling her forward and rushing her up the steps. She would have to leave the guards to their fate.

10

DRAGON MASTER

The sun was finally rising as the stolen horse galloped away from the fort of Dragon Hold.

"Where will we go?" Olwen asked. Her voice was strong: it was a voice Andra thought she'd never hear again.

"Gilde's temple, they shouldn't find us there." She held her lover tight, as if she were still broken, yet she was as vibrant as ever; strong, magnificent. Her warm scent filled Andra's nostrils; she had thought she would never hold again and now she would never let her go.

"No," Olwen said suddenly, as she turned in the saddle to face Andra. "They will find Gilde's body in the hold and there are too many who know where she kept worship. They'll find us."

Andra pulled the reins and the horse slowed to a trot. "Where, then?"

Olwen looked up at her as she reclined in her arms. There was a smile on her lips; it was strange to see her now with those gold eyes like the dragon that had saved her life. Andra wondered if the dragon still lived, if any of the guards had survived that strange attack, and what it was that Gilde had unleashed. What they had both unleashed. There was no going back for that dead boy now. No going back for any of them. She had wanted to save a life tonight.

The cost of that life had been high.

She didn't realise she had turned to look at the distant hill fort until Olwen pulled at her chin and turned her back.

"You saved me," Olwen whispered, stroking the soft skin of Andra's wounded cheek. "You came after me, even after everything, even after you warned me, you knew it was a mistake, I knocked you down and yet..." Olwen seemed to be looking into her very soul, taking all of her in.

"Of course." Andra felt a swell of guilt rise in her at the memory of her indecision. But she suppressed it; she knew her decision was made the moment Olwen was struck down, the decisions had become costlier but there had only ever been one course of action. "I am nothing without you." She took Olwen's hand and kissed the soft skin, hot to her touch, full of life. "I would have gone to the underworld and fought the guards of death itself to bring you back."

"It almost feels as though you did." Olwen looked at her own hands, opening and closing them as if amazed she still possessed them.

"What was it like?"

"Dying?"

"Being dead."

"I..." her eyes searched her memory, "I don't remember, at least if there is anything to remember about death." She smiled suddenly. "But I do remember life. A thousand lives."

"What do you mean?"

"The Dragons, Andra, I felt them all, every one of them." She laughed. "We did it, I crossed the threshold; I entered the realm of dragons. I heard them in my mind and

I was as strong as all of them at once!" She shivered, and her smile was gone. Andra held her a little tighter. "But it seems I am strong no more."

"You are the strongest woman I have ever known." The horse stopped as they came to the crossroads. "Which way?"

"Home."

"To Dragon Hold? But Olwen, you saw the chaos in there, the dragon, half the guards are dead, Gilde… We can't just walk back into the fort—"

"If we run we look guilty."

"We are guilty!"

"Of what?" Olwen looked at her. "No one will even be able to guess at what we have achieved. We did it, Andra, we tapped into the power of the Gods! You brought me back from the dead! And now you wish to hide away in a mould-infested, old ruin?"

"But you are back to me now. This is our chance to run, to live out our lives together and away from all this—"

"To hide? To cower in the dark? Afraid of every creak? Every shadow? No, Andra, I'll not live like that anymore."

"They'll think you dead, Olwen. They'll not come after us. We're finally free."

"And what of all the other Druids?"

"What?"

"We might be free, but all other Druids still live in servitude to that dragon. My family did not die for us to run."

Andra shook her head. "What would you have me do?"

Olwen laughed. "We have achieved exactly what that accursed Dwarf wanted so desperately to prevent. She will not be able to stop me now. No one will."

"She killed you before, she'll kill you again."

"I won't make the same mistake twice."

"Blast it, Olwen! Going back to Dragon Hold is making the same mistake twice."

Olwen slid down off the horse. She didn't turn back to Andra. Instead, she started making her way along the road back to the fort on the hill.

"Please, don't. It's too dangerous!"

"If we give up now, then it's all been for nothing." She turned back with rage upon her lips. "They win, Andra. They get to keep magic for themselves. If we run and hide, then every time one of our people dies for want of healing, the fault will be ours. Every time the crops fail, the fault will be ours. Every time a herd stops giving milk – every encroachment of our border! Those damned wizards deny us our birthright and this is my chance—our chance to wrest power back from them. I will destroy the wizard's grip on power, and I will destroy the dragon's hold over the Druids." She held out her hand. "Come with me?"

"You intend to destroy the Gods, Olwen."

"I intend to master them."

Andra shook her head. "Is that even possible?"

She shrugged and smiled. "I've seen into the minds of dragons, Andra, I know it can be done."

Andra sighed and closed her eyes. It didn't matter whether it could be done or not. She was with Olwen to the end. She nodded. "Then let's go home."

Olwen smiled and Andra helped her back onto the horse as they turned and headed to Dragon Hold with the morning sun warming their backs.

"Good." Olwen rested her head against Andra's chest. "I'd hate to conquer the world alone."

THE END

DRAGON WHISPER

A LOOMING WAR. A DEVASTATING BLIGHT. A GOD HUNGRY FOR SOULS.

To save herself, she will first have to save the world.

In the dying forests of the Weald Wood, Breanna, a young outcast, is simply trying to earn a Hunter's axe.

When she witnesses the sacred Forest Drake kill her father and destroy her village home, she knows her life is forever altered. But Breanna holds a secret that could be the key to stopping the Ancient Dragon God's rampage.

The fate of every being in the land now depends on one young woman who can hear the Dragon's Whisper.

Will she find her courage, or see her world destroyed?

Dragon Whisper marks the beginning of a queer, epic fantasy set in a land of Dark Wizards and Warrior Queens for fans of Game of Thrones, Skyrim, and kick-ass women who love women... <u>*continue the adventure*</u>

ABOUT THE AUTHOR

Niamh Murphy is an author of adventure books with lesbian main characters. Her mission is to write exciting and engaging stories with women taking centre stage.

She is passionate about experimenting with different genres and has a fondness for romance, as well as action-adventure. She has written stories with vampires, were-wolves, elves, magic, knights, sorceresses, and witches as well as contemporary and humorous stories, but always with a lesbian protagonist and a romantic element to the tale.

Read more about her, and find exclusive free content, at AuthorNiamh.com

Printed in Great Britain
by Amazon